the
christmas eve
storyteller

the Christmas Eve Storyteller

written & illustrated by

EDWARD HAYS

FOREST OF PEACE BOOKS

OTHER BOOKS BY THE AUTHOR:
(available from the publisher)

Prayers and Rituals

Prayers for a Planetary Pilgrim
Prayers for the Domestic Church
Prayers for the Servants of God

Parables and Stories

St. George and the Dragon
The Magic Lantern
The Ethiopian Tattoo Shop
Twelve and One-Half Keys
Sundancer

Contemporary Spirituality

Holy Fools & Mad Hatters
A Pilgrim's Almanac
In Pursuit of the Great White Rabbit
Pray All Ways
Secular Sanctity

THE CHRISTMAS EVE STORYTELLER

copyright © 1992, by Edward M. Hays

Library of Congress Catalog Card Number: 92-73009
ISBN 0-939516-16-0

published by
Forest of Peace Books, Inc.
PO Box 269
Leavenworth, KS 66048-0269 U.S.A.

printed by
Hall Directory, Inc.
Topeka, KS 66608

first printing: August 1992
second printing: November 1992

cover art and illustrations by
Edward Hays

Dedicated

to

Father Paul Miller

a friend with a Christmas heart

TABLE OF CONTENTS

'TWAS THE NIGHT
BEFORE CHRISTMAS...

The night was bitter cold. I remember it so well, even though it was many years ago. The fingers of the icy winter wind pulled with all their force at our house, which clung tightly to its old stone foundation. The snap and crackle of the burning logs seemed to sing a reassuring song: "Child, fear not the storm outside. You are safe in this warm circle of love." This night was, for me and my family, the most wonderful of nights: Christmas Eve – and this particular Christmas Eve was to be especially magical!

I looked out the window, watching the wind blowing the snow, whipping it downward in great white clouds over the edge of our roof with its row of icicles which hung like long, jagged dragon teeth. I tried to extend the range of my vision beyond the blowing snow, but the night was so dark. It was far too black for me to see much past the small patch of light that peeked through the window onto the snow below. "Maybe," I thought, "I may see Santa Claus. Perhaps, just perhaps, he will come tonight on Christmas Eve." Sometimes he did come late at night, and then on other years he came very early on Christmas morning.

Although it was long ago, I still recall how I had patiently counted the days until Christmas. Each morning, as soon as I was dressed, I would go to the calendar that hung on the kitchen wall to count the remaining days. Standing on one of the kitchen table chairs, I would take my mother's shopping-list pencil and with a broad stroke would cross off another day. Those days from Thanksgiving till Christmas passed so slowly. To me, as a child, they seemed to shuffle along like old Mrs. Koenig, who took forever to make her way down the aisle in church to go to Holy Communion.

Finally, the days of waiting had each come and gone. Tonight was Christmas Eve! I left my sentry's post at the front window and joined my little brothers in front of the Christmas crib which was next to the Christmas tree. The dime store stable, transformed by the glow of the Christmas tree lights, became strikingly beautiful. The cardboard palm trees and the plaster camel next to the Wise Men, illuminated by the tree's lights, took on the magical wonder of some far-off land. I was about to change the position of one of the shepherds, the one with a sheep on his shoulders, when a loud knock came at our front door.

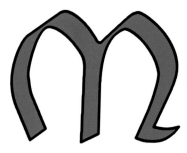 brothers and I looked at each other with large eyes. Could it be, could it really be that *he* had arrived? Never before had he come when we were awake! Together we raced behind our father as he went to the front door, certain that it was Santa Claus. My father opened the door to a winter whirlwind of snow and icy cold as we boys looked up in wonder. The figure standing at our door was so tall that he filled the doorway, and he was clothed in snow from head to foot.

"Friend, I fear I've lost my way. May I come in and warm myself?" The stranger's voice was deep, as measured as a waltz and warm, even for one who was blanketed with snow.

"Come in, please," said father, ushering the man inside. "Come in and warm yourself." As the snow-covered mountain stepped across our threshold, my father quickly closed the door in the face of the raging beast of a storm. A miniature snowstorm fell about us as father helped remove the large overcoat from the stranger who was stomping his feet free of snow.

"Mother," sang out father, "we have a surprise guest. Bring him a cup of coffee, please, for he must be near frozen." Guiding our guest toward the fire, he said, "Come over here, sir, by the fire. You must be chilled to the bone. It's a bad night to be out—and a worse one to be lost."

REMOVING his cap, the tall stranger shook his head free of snow. At first I thought it was too stubborn to fall away, but then I realized that it wasn't all snow. Most of it was hair! Besides a head of great white hair, he had bushy white eyebrows and a full beard. All his hair flowed outward like the rays of a bleached sun and highlighted his skin which was pink from the cold. Standing by the fire, he slowly pulled off his gloves to reveal the longest fingers I had ever seen.

"Blessings on you, friend, and on all this house, for your kindness to a stranger," he said as he sat down in a chair by the fire.

"This is a holy night, sir. There are no strangers on Christmas Eve," returned my father with a broad smile.

The surprise of the visit and the unusual appearance of the tall stranger had caused me to forget about Santa Claus—but not my little brother Tommy.

"We thought you were Santa Claus," he said with a disappointed tone. "Did you see him out there?"

"No son, but I'm sure he's on the way. You see, lads, snow and sleet don't slow down Santa Claus like they do us kind of folk."

"Children, time for bed," said my mother as my older sister handed a cup of hot coffee to the stranger. "Tomorrow's Christmas, and. . . ."

"Please, please, Mom, can't we stay up a little longer? Maybe the stranger knows a story he can tell us," I pleaded.

 STORY, indeed! I know many stories, and it's truly a marvel that you should ask for one. You see, it's an ancient custom to repay the kindness of a host by sharing a story. Your parents have been kind enough to give me shelter from the storm on this bitter night. The least I can do is spin you a yarn or two."

My father smiled at my mother, tilting his head slightly to the right as he often did when he wanted her to go along with him. She smiled back and nodded in agreement, permitting the exception.

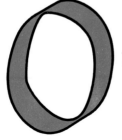**NLY** when I was older and understood a bit more about life did I realize the great gift the stranger gave my parents and us on that Christmas Eve night. When I was a child, times were hard, and the Christmas gifts for my sister and us boys were scarce. No extra money in those days meant few surprises or treats under the tree. On that Christmas Eve long ago, however, the offer of the Storyteller to spin some yarns more than made up for what Santa didn't bring. I've celebrated many a Christmas in my life, but that was the most magical and memorable of them all.

We boys sat on the floor around the stranger's chair, while my sister and folks pulled their chairs up close to his. The fire crackled merrily in the background as the tiny lights flickering on the Christmas tree cast a rainbow aura over the room. Setting down his coffee cup, the stranger raised his right hand in the air, and we all fell into a silence full of anticipation. Without a word, he began to move his long fingers gracefully through the air. It looked like he was indeed weaving some invisible garment as he began to spin his yarns.

Pointing to a picture of Santa Claus on a Christmas card which lay on the table, he smiled and asked me, "Do you know why Santa's so jolly and fat? I can see by your eyes that you don't. Well, this story begins with a good and holy saint by the name of Nicholas. Let me tell you how that all came about, long, long ago."

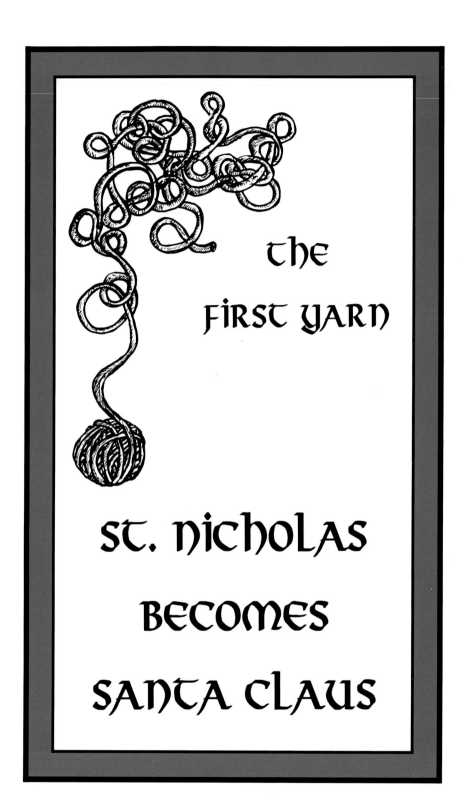

THE
FIRST YARN

ST. NICHOLAS
BECOMES
SANTA CLAUS

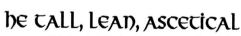

The tall, lean, ascetical Bishop Nicholas arrived in the new world together with a boatload of other Dutch immigrants. Old Bishop Nicholas was such a good man that everyone called him Saint Nicholas. He was loved by children and adults alike, even if he was a bit stern and pious.

One fair day, he was walking along the road alone when a black coach drawn by four black horses came thundering down the road. When the foreboding carriage and its dark steeds reached him, it suddenly came to a halt. Three hooded figures leaped out of the coach and seized the aged bishop. They quickly dragged him into the coach and, shouting an order to the driver, whisked him to an old farmhouse hidden way back in the hills.

Once they had secured him inside the old house, the kidnappers confronted him. The conspirators were actually colonial businessmen, New England shopkeepers. Using threats, they insisted that St. Nicholas tell them his secret. "Tell us," they demanded of the old saint, "what is the secret of your popularity at the holiday season? Why are the children so fond of you?"

The aged bishop pressed his lips tightly together, shook his head from left to right and refused to answer. No matter how much they threatened him, he was resolute in his silence.

The kidnappers then attempted various forms of torture to get him to talk. First they tried to pry the secret out of him by months of solitary confinement, but to no avail. The saintly bishop loved the solitude, telling his captors that he had always longed to be a hermit.

is kidnappers now changed tactics and began to torture him with starvation! Each day for months all they gave him was bread and water. He didn't complain. In fact, he loved it. He told them that he had always wanted to do a long penance with a Black Fast. Because of this punishment, St. Nicholas was now lean as a fence post, but his lips were sealed about his secret.

At this, his captors held a meeting in the kitchen of the farmhouse to decide what they could do to make St. Nicholas talk. The leader of the gang slammed his fist on the kitchen table, saying, "He's a saint! We try to starve him to death, and he only calls it a fast! We lock him up in solitary confinement, and he calls it desert solitude. What are we going to do?"

"I've got it," cried one of the merchant captors who proceeded to share his new form of torture with his co-conspirators.

"Yes, yes, that's the way to pry out the secret of his popularity at the holiday season," they all shouted gleefully.

Beginning the very next day they brought a collection of musicians, singers, jesters and clowns to the farmhouse. Day and night—with the bishop's hands tied to a chair so he couldn't hold them over his ears — they tortured the saint. For hours on end the musicians played and sang merry songs. Then the clowns performed funny acts and told him endless jokes. The saint screamed for mercy, but no mercy was shown. In fact, this was only the first wave of their new torture.

The second phase of their vicious plan was to force-feed him slices of mouth-watering pink roast beef, gallons of plum pudding and hot chestnuts roasted on an open fire. The cruel merchants forced Saint Nicholas to eat five full meals a day, as well as a snack before bedtime. When he refused, they placed a funnel in his mouth and stuffed him like a goose being readied for market.

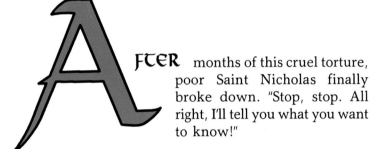

AFTER months of this cruel torture, poor Saint Nicholas finally broke down. "Stop, stop. All right, I'll tell you what you want to know!"

Eagerly the captors encircled the saint, rubbing their greasy palms in excitement. The bloated, bedraggled bishop was only able to whisper a few words.

"Louder, you papist!" shouted the shopkeepers. "What's your secret?"

"My secret," whispered St. Nicholas, whose white beard was full of cookie crumbs and sticky clots of honey, "my secret is that the greatest joy in life is in giving gifts! And those who give are counted among the most beloved of all. The secret is *gift-giving*."

Well, friends, that's how the Christmas Season was

born. The New England merchants lived happily ever after and, I might add, richly ever after. You may think that the story ends here, but don't forget about the holy hostage, St. Nicholas.

 AVING forced out his secret, the shopkeeper captors raced off to the city, leaving St. Nicholas alone in the old farmhouse. During his imprisonment he had worn only his long underwear. Now that he was free to leave, he went looking for his bishop's robes. Finding nothing downstairs, he climbed into the attic of the farm house.

At the top of the attic steps the first thing he saw was a tall, oval mirror. Poor St. Nicholas glanced at his image and couldn't believe what he saw! He was so fat that his belly looked like a fifty pound sack of sugar! His beard, which once had been trimmed neatly, was now long and bushy. The endless hours of being tortured by having to listen to music and merriment had changed even his facial appearance! His face no longer was piously stern. It now wore a permanent broad and jolly smile. Even his eyes, once downcast with humility, now danced with mirth.

As he looked in the mirror, he realized that even if he found his bishop's robes, they would no longer fit him. What was he to do? He couldn't leave the house wearing only his white long underwear. Then he spied an old trunk in the far end of the attic. Inside, he found a red Dutch farmer's suit and cap trimmed with white fur, a large black belt and a pair of leather knee boots. To his surprise, they fit perfectly. He walked out of the farmhouse a free man and, according to local legend, left New England for far-off places.

The most reliable accounts say that the escaped bishop went to the far North as a missionary to the elves. For years he labored there to convert them from their pagan ways and naughty habits of playing little tricks on humans. Like a good missionary, he not only converted them, he also taught them a productive trade—toymaking! It also seems that he fell in love and married a wonderful woman who wanted to share his life. Nothing more is known about him until the middle of the nineteenth century.

**URING** the mid-1800's St. Nick returned to America and his old occupation of bringing gifts to children. His nighttime visits were not on December 6th, which had been his customary day for gift-giving, but on Christmas Eve or on the very feast of the Christ Child's birth. Whenever he was seen, which was rarely, he was not dressed as a bishop. He wore instead the red suit and boots he had found in the farmhouse attic. Also, he now traveled in a wondrous sleigh. Further, his name had been slightly changed from the original Dutch. No longer was he known as Santa Nic'Claus, but now as Santa Claus.

"Another one! Tell us another," my sister, brothers and I pleaded in unison, having been delighted by the first story.

"Ah, lads and lass, indeed, there are more yarns to spin. If your good parents don't mind, and you're willin', there's enough to spin you to sleep. Have you heard the old story about the elf who saved Santa's sleigh?"

"No, please tell it to us," I said. And so, the Christmas Eve Storyteller told us the tale of the little old elf who helped Santa with his great dilemma—and following that, wove us a whole tapestry of other tales.

THE SECOND YARN

THE ELF WHO SAVED CHRISTMAS

At the end of a long Christmas day many years ago, as the North Pole glistened under a full moon, a tired and frustrated Santa Claus finally returned home from his gift-giving journey. As the elves helped him remove the harnesses from his weary reindeer, Santa said, "Little friends, we must do something! Each year my journey takes longer." He lovingly stroked his reindeer and softly said, "So many children were disappointed because we arrived so late at their homes. You did your best, I know. And you too, my great sleigh!"

And what a grand sleigh it was! It had been given to Santa Claus by its original owner, Czar Nicholas I of Russia. The imperial sleigh was painted in rich reds and yellows, with hand-carved decorations covered with real gold. On the sides of the sleigh were brightly colored images of Saint Nicholas, the Madonna and Child and several other saints. They all had real gold halos, and precious jewels sparkled from the designs on their clothing. So wondrous was this magnificent sleigh that those lucky enough to see it were held spellbound by its splendorous beauty.

Long, long ago, when Santa Claus first began to make his Christmas Eve visits, his splendid sleigh raced like lightning across the snow-covered hills and fields. Of course, in those olden days there were fewer people on earth, and so the sleigh was less weighted down with presents. As the world's population grew, however, the sleigh became heavier. As more and more parts of the earth were settled, it became impossible to visit every home on a single night. Each year Santa returned home to the North Pole later and later. Each year more and more children had to wait for the arrival of their beloved but tardy Santa Claus.

After Santa had rested from his long Christmas Eve ride across the earth, he called a community meeting of all those who worked at the North Pole. They met in the great barn next to his house. The oak beams which crisscrossed the ceiling like intertwined tree branches were covered with carvings of birds, beasts and flowers. Santa stood in his magnificent sleigh, with Mrs. Claus seated beside him, and addressed the crowd of elves: "My friends, we must find a new way to visit all the homes on earth in one night."

"You could get an airplane; that would be faster," said one of the elves. But at this suggestion the reindeer snorted and pawed the ground in disapproval, and a groan rose up from the crowd of elves. Mrs. Claus spoke up, "True, an airplane would be faster, but it wouldn't have the same magical touch as our magnificent sleigh and beautiful reindeer."

SANTA nodded: "Yes, I agree. But I may have to travel by plane to reach every home on Christmas Eve. I hate to think of it, yet we may have to face reality and retire the reindeer and my sleigh. But are there any other ideas?" The meeting lasted till almost lunch time as many members of the North Pole community expressed their concerns and fears. Santa ended it, saying, "We have almost a year to find a good solution. I'm sure we can solve this problem together."

As Santa, Mrs. Claus and the crowd of elves left the barn, one old elf with a long white beard remained

behind, leaning on his carved wooden staff. Because he had anticipated the reason for the community meeting, the elf brought along some plans to address Santa's dilemma. Although he had listened to all the ideas proposed, he could not muster up enough confidence to say anything at the meeting. The old elf's green coat which reached almost to the floor had large, deep pockets that once had been filled with presents. Long ago, just like Santa, he had been as well known as St. Nick in Germany. His name was the Birthday Elf, and he visited children on their birthdays, bearing beautiful gifts. But with the passage of time he was forgotten; now retired, he lived in the Old Elf Home behind Santa's house.

The aged elf spoke to the great sleigh, "I hope that what has been my fate doesn't also become yours."

The regal sleigh only laughed. Glowing with pride, the sleigh said, "That's impossible; part of the joy of Christmas is for people to see me. Christmas wouldn't be Christmas without Santa arriving in me!"

The old elf replied, "I wouldn't be so sure. I never thought I'd only be a faint memory of what I once was. But look at me: it can happen to you too!"

Touched, the magnificent sleigh answered, "Birthday Elf, once upon a time, like Santa, you also gave gifts that brought children delight. Only you gave them presents on their birthdays instead of Christmas. You may be retired now, but I'm sure you haven't lost your magical power. I know you can conjure up some way for me to travel faster and further than I do now, so that

I can continue to be the one who carries Santa Claus. Please show me the plans that you brought with you."

The Birthday Elf's heart pounded with excitement at the thought of once again being the agent of answered dreams. "All right," he said, "let me see if the old magic is still alive in me." Unrolling the scroll of paper he was carrying, he revealed a detailed drawing of Santa's sleigh, complete with wheels mounted on its runners. As the reindeer looked on, he explained that the sleigh could travel much faster on wheels, that they would be ideal for those places without snow.

The reindeer and great sleigh all shouted with glee, "Wonderful, Birthday Elf! That's the solution to our problem. Take your idea to Santa and see what he thinks."

SO the old elf went to see Santa Claus and showed him the sketch. Santa carefully studied the design and said, "Good idea, Birthday Elf! It would help me cover more miles in less time. But I don't think we can save enough time to make all my many stops in one day. Thank you, but I believe we need a more radical solution."

Discouraged, the old elf returned to the barn and told the sleigh and the reindeer what Santa had said. They too were disappointed, but the Birthday Elf promised to try again.

Weeks passed and months slipped by, until it was mid-June. Everyone at the North Pole knew that it was only six months until the time for Santa to begin his Christmas Eve journey. For now their worry was covered over by the feasting and gladness of midsummer's eve. All the elves celebrated with great bonfires and dancing. The Birthday Elf, however, was not with them. He was in the barn with the sleigh. Unrolling another large scroll of paper, he said, "On this most magical of nights, I come to you with my best idea yet. It's the grandest gift I can give you." The reindeer peered with puzzled eyes at a strange drawing of the sleigh, which looked like it had come from the pen of Leonardo da Vinci. In the center of the sleigh was a network of gears and pulleys that operated a shaft which engaged a revolving system of propellers. "My idea," said the aged elf, "is to convert you into a magnificent flying sleigh!"

"Marvelous," shouted the sleigh and reindeer, "that's surely the solution. With this design we should easily cover the whole world in a single night. Take it to Santa right away."

And so the Birthday Elf went to the midsummer's eve celebration and called Santa Claus aside to show him the plans. While Santa liked the idea, he was concerned that all the machinery necessary to engage the propellers wouldn't leave much room for all his gifts. But he nodded approval and told his elf engineers to begin work on it the very next morning.

By mid-September the flying sleigh was ready to be tested. The reindeer were harnessed up and Santa climbed aboard. All the elves gathered along the runway to watch the test flight. Mrs. Claus waved a red flag to give the signal, and when Santa threw the switch the propellers began to whirl, as the reindeer raced down the runway. To a chorus of cheering elves, the sleigh rose from the ground and began to gain altitude. Santa smiled and the sleigh swelled with pride as they started to soar upward. But then suddenly they began to lose altitude. A great groan descended on the crowd of elves, as Santa, the sleigh and the reindeer fell quickly back to earth after flying only a short distance.

Mrs. Claus and all the elves came running to the sleigh where a disappointed Santa sat shaking his head. "I had hoped it would work, but we were too heavy to fly.

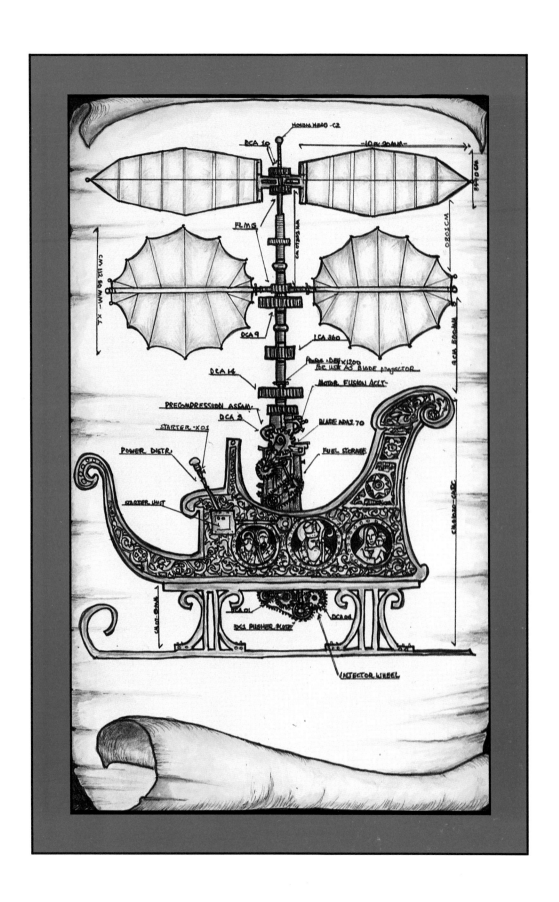

Sorry, Birthday Elf, it was a good try, but not quite a radical enough solution! Still, we need to find an answer soon. There are only three months till Christmas!"

As the crowd slowly slipped away, the Birthday Elf was left standing next to the magnificent sleigh. He kept repeating, "I don't understand." Then, turning to the sleigh, he added, "According to my calculations the combined weight of sleigh, Santa, the gifts and the reindeer shouldn't have kept my invention from working. I need time to think." With that, the elf withdrew to the solitude of his room.

O**N** Thanksgiving night, the Birthday Elf entered the darkened barn, carrying a small lantern. The light from his lantern cast long yellow rays upward onto the arched oaken beams. The wondrous—but now worried—sleigh asked eagerly, "Have you brought me the gift I desire most?"

After a long pause the old elf answered, "Well, yes and no." The reindeer awoke and eagerly raised their ears.

"Yes and no?" repeated the sleigh. "What does that mean? And I see that you've come empty-handed this time. Have you no gift for me?"

"Whether what I have brought is a gift or not all depends upon you," answered the old elf. "I have spent many sleepless nights thinking about what went wrong with my last idea. I have also pondered on Santa's words—remember when he said that what was needed was a radical solution? I believe this time I have an answer, a radical one." With that he removed from his pocket a single page which had been torn from a book.

The page shined brightly even in the faint light of his small lantern as he handed it to the sleigh.

"Where is this page from?" asked the sleigh.

"I tore it out of Santa's Bible," answered the old elf. "It's a gift that holds the secret to your fondest dreams." And the elf held his lantern high so that the sleigh could read the words from the 8th chapter of St. Paul's Second Letter to the Corinthians:

> You are well acquainted with the favor
> shown you by our Lord Jesus Christ;
> how for your sake he made himself poor
> though he was rich, so that you might
> become rich by his poverty.

"I don't understand," said the sleigh, "what does this have to do with me or our problem?"

The old, white-bearded elf responded, "The answer is hidden in that single sentence. But you'll have to find it yourself or it won't be the answer. Great problems are resolved only by radical answers, and, my friend, no one likes to think radical ideas. Good night, and good luck!" The Birthday Elf slowly walked out into the night. The north wind, already heavy with snow, rattled through the rafters of the great barn as the magnificent sleigh pored over the puzzling sentence, repeating it again and again.

On December 6th, the feast of St. Nicholas, the sun transformed the snow and ice into a crystal world which sparkled with blinding beauty. Led by the Birthday Elf, all the elves processed to Santa's front door singing "Happy Birthday." Santa and Mrs. Claus came to the door to grcct thcm. Beaming with joy, the Birthday Elf said, "Santa, I bring you the best of all birthday gifts. Come with us to the great barn."

When they arrived at the doors of the barn, the Birthday Elf turned and said to the crowd, "A surprise awaits you. Be prepared." As he swung open the great doors, the sunlight flooded the barn in a yellow river of light. In the center of the wave of light was Santa's sleigh. Next to it was a paint can and a large brush. The great sleigh had been painted entirely in a drab green! It looked no different from a common farmer's sleigh. A gasp of horror rose from Santa and the elves who crowded around him.

"What's happened to my magnificent sleigh?" moaned Santa.

"I did it myself, Santa," answered the sleigh. "Now I'm ready to carry you and your gifts anywhere in the world, and we can do it all in a single night. I can fly now, without the need for any complicated machinery. I've painted myself plain green because I've discovered that what made us too heavy was my pride in being the most splendorous sleigh in all the world. I had to become poor in order to be the bearer of you and your gifts."

On that birthday feast of St. Nicholas there was another test flight. Only this time Santa, his sleigh and reindeer easily took off and sailed into the sky. Again and again they circled the North Pole, as the elves and Mrs. Claus danced and cheered gleefully below. The heart of the now drab-green sleigh had never known such joy. Santa, with his great beard blowing behind him like a white silk scarf, merrily waved to his friends on the ground. His face beaming with joy, Santa repeated aloud the words of the Birthday Elf, "'Great problems are solved only by radical answers.' Ah, the whole mystery of Christmas is repeated again!"

THE
THIRD YARN

THE STAR

PERHAPS AT NO OTHER TIME
of the year are there more
pageants, programs and shows
performed by both amateurs and
professionals than during the
Christmas holidays. From schools and churches to the
stars of stage, screen and television, all have their holiday programs. This is a story about one very special
Christmas pageant.

The backstage dressing room was crowded with
members of the cast busy adding the final touches to
their makeup. Among them was a host of young per-
formers who longed someday to be famous stars. Each
secretly wished that the big stars of the production would
catch a cold or oversleep so they could have a chance
to step into the limelight.

ONE YOUNG ACTRESS with
sandy-colored hair was ad-
justing her star beams as she
hummed, *There's No Business
Like Show Business.* Her starry-
eyed musings were interrupted by a loud knock at the
door followed by the instruction, "On stage, everyone!"

They all eagerly trooped out on stage where the director was engaged in a heated discussion with the orchestra leader.

"I don't know the *precise* time when we'll begin. How can I?"

"Then how are all my musicians to keep their instruments in tune if we have to sit around here and wait until . . . ."

"Well, I'm sorry, but that's the way it is! We both know that's not our decision to make. We know it'll be soon, but the exact timing is in the hands of the Producer. Just tell your musicians to keep their instruments in tune as best they can. How to do that is your problem, not mine. I've got enough problems of my own—like this chorus line."

Shaking his head, the frustrated orchestra leader went down into the orchestra pit. The director shouted over the noise, "Quiet, everyone! Quiet on stage! Cast, take your places, please. Lights! Music! OK, stars, light up and start dancing!"

The houselights dimmed and the music swelled as the young sandy-haired actress along with the others in the chorus line of stars turned their lights up to full intensity. The effect was both blinding and beautiful as the orchestra thundered out the overture theme, *Hark the herald, angels sing . . . .*

"Stop...Stop!" shouted the director. "Angels, that's your

cue! Wake up, you're supposed to start singing. Please, everyone pay attention to your cues. Again, Maestro, from the top of the page."

Hark the herald, angels sing; glory to the newborn king, rang out the chorus of angels floating overhead as the chorus line of stars danced in circles below.

hen the overture concluded, it was time for the star of the show to appear. And appear she did! The sandy-haired actress watched in awe as the star floated out onto the stage. The aspiring star thought to herself, "She's more radiant than any of us here. She's pure talent, grace and beauty."

The director nodded to the star with respect; then, turning, he bellowed out, "All right, everyone in your places. Lights, music...let's go!"

The music soared, the angels sang and the stars danced as *the* star pirouetted, spinning round and round like a top. Rainbows of colored light streaked out from her in all directions. The rehearsal continued until, exhausted, every one retired for the night.

That night, in her small room, the young sandy-haired actress prayed, "O You who created us, who hears the prayers of each of your creatures, even us small and in-significant ones, grant me the gift to become a great star."

Before climbing into bed, she pirouetted in imitation

of the star's performance earlier that day at rehearsal. She strained to open her heart completely so that all the colors hidden there could burst forth in splendor. For one fleeting moment she forgot herself, even her feet which always seemed to fail to do what she wanted them to, and she *became* the dance. Lost in the wonder of her dancing, she became absolutely radiant.

Exhausted, she collapsed on her bed, but her heart was throbbing so hard that she couldn't go to sleep. She tried, knowing she needed her rest since the next night might be Opening Night. Gradually, the big bass drum in her heart became a whisper, and she slipped into sleep, but only to dream of being a great star.

In the morning, the entire cast, chorus and orchestra went through another rehearsal. The director, perhaps more earnestly than usual, told them to be ready, for that very night the show might go on! The day dragged on, but finally night descended upon the stage. Worn out by the anticipation and a lack of sleep, the sandy-haired actress and several others had fallen asleep. They were suddenly awakened by excited shouts, "On stage, everyone, the Producer says tonight's *the* night!"

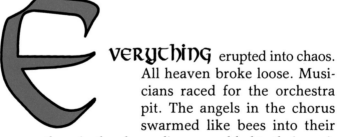

EVERYTHING erupted into chaos. All heaven broke loose. Musicians raced for the orchestra pit. The angels in the chorus swarmed like bees into their places as those in the chorus line scrambled to their positions on the great stage high above the earth. Down below, all was stillness as Planet Earth lay sleeping, covered with darkness. It was in this peaceful setting that the entire cast coordinated their final preparations high in the sky over a little town in Palestine.

"Five minutes! Everyone stand by! We're about to begin. Where's the star?" shouted the director.

"She's not in her dressing room, Michael. We've looked everywhere and can't find her. I don't know where she is."

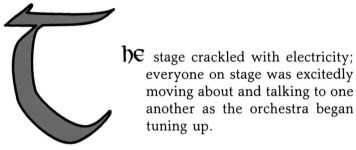 stage crackled with electricity; everyone on stage was excitedly moving about and talking to one another as the orchestra began tuning up.

"Quiet on stage! Everyone, quiet," screamed the director over the bedlam of noise. "No time left now to try to find her! Who here can be her stand-in? Do any of you in the chorus line know her part?"

"I do," said the sandy-haired actress, her voice as soft as a snowflake.

"You with the sandy hair," demanded the director, "you in the back row of the chorus line, did you say you know her routine? Come quickly! We don't have a minute to spare."

Standing in front of the director and all the cast, the would-be star felt so small, so inadequate. On the other hand, she knew it was the chance of a lifetime, even if her knees were shaking so badly that she could hardly stand — let alone dance.

"OK, kid, looks like you're the only chance we've got. I hope you've got what it takes because this production is a one-and-only show! We'll never get a second try."

She took one deep breath after another. Her heart was still pounding, and so she closed her eyes and prayed with all the passion she could gather up, "My Holy Creator, fill me with your Spirit. Fill me with your light and love."

"Fifteen seconds and counting. 5-4-3-2 — OK, Maestro, music...." With an upraised arm, Michael the Archangel signaled all the angels to their places. Then, turning to the sandy-haired actress, he said, "OK, kid, just do it!"

Hark the herald, angels sing; glory to the newborn king. Peace on earth and mercy mild; God and sinners reconciled.... Eyes closed, she whirled as never before. To her amazement as she spun round, rainbow-colored light streaked forth from her heart, sending bits and pieces of her brilliance billions of miles out into space.

Joyful, all ye nations rise. Join the triumph of the skies.... The young star was in ecstasy as all the cells in her body, like strings of firecrackers, exploded into radiant light. Each blazing cell gave a farewell kiss and then raced downward in a cascading waterfall of liquid light onto that little stable outside Bethlehem.

The music continued to saturate the boundless night air: *With angelic host proclaim, "Christ is born in Bethlehem...."*

Flight after flight of angels wove in and out of the waterfall of her star-shower, singing in full voice their song of hope and peace to the poor shepherds looking up into the night sky. Open-mouthed, they stood gaping at her as she exploded right over their heads. Behind the emerging star all the rest of the stars in the universe whirled in pinwheels of splendor.

Hark the herald, angels sing; glory to the newborn king.... As bits and pieces of her very body went streaking out across the world and out into the universe, she saw something far off over the edge of the eastern horizon. Three wise astronomers were jumping up and down in ecstatic applause at her performance.

As much as she wanted to surrender to the music and explode in absolute brilliance, she held back. She resisted spending all of herself, for she knew she had to conserve what little energy was left for the finale – until all, yes everyone, had seen the Sign.

As the orchestra and chorus sounded the last note, the young star knew that she had made it to the finale. With one final whirl, she poured forth every last piece of her self. Suddenly, all was blackness, for the great stage curtain had descended. Exhausted, emptied but proud, she collapsed, knowing that she had done it. She had been *the* Star!

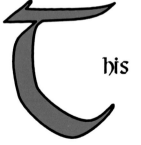his is *not* **The End**, however. Oh, no, for "The show must go on." And it does, again and again, for those with eyes to see. Go outside on Christmas Eve, on any of the twelve nights of Christmas – or any night – and look up into the night sky. I promise you, if you look carefully, you will see her, the Star of that First Christmas Show.

She's there among all the brilliant ones, for stars never die! Even when with glory and splendor they blaze forth and steal the show, they never die! Believe me, after a brief rest in their dressing rooms, they once again gather up the stuff of greatness and walk out on the darkened stage of space. With the same brilliance of the First Christmas Show, they dance again for all to see. You and I need only humble hearts, like those of the simple shepherds of Bethlehem, to have front-row seats.

the
FOURTH YARN

the gift
of the
magi

Nce upon a time three Oriental kings made a star-guided journey, carrying with them three gifts. Their gifts are perhaps the most famous in all history: gold, frankincense and myrrh. After they had presented them to the mysterious infant king lying in the stable where the star had led them, they returned home by a different route. As the three kings traveled homeward, each carried a souvenir of his star-journey carefully hidden from the others.

When they stopped the first night on their way home, their attendants pitched the silk pavilions and made camp. As the crescent moon appeared in the west, they finished their supper and retired. Even the camel drivers were asleep and all was silent. King Balthasar, however, sat alone in his tent, in the glow of a brass lamp, reflecting on the gift of gold he had given the God-King in Bethlehem. He smiled at himself for the need he had felt to take something, a small token of remembrance, from that insignificant stable where the infant lay.

By the light of the lamp he opened a golden case and removed a single piece of yellow straw, saying aloud, "I came on this quest to seek a king, a real king, because I did not feel kingly. I have always doubted my royalty. What makes me different from my camel drivers? Do I not also have the same needs for food and drink, for love and physical comfort as they? How is a king different, after all, from a carpenter or any commoner?"

Slowly he held the straw up to the light as he mused, "I, Balthasar, followed the star, seeking a God-King to confirm my own kingship, for are not all crowns made of cardboard and all thrones of straw?" He replaced the straw in its precious case and continued, "Back in Bethlehem, the father of that child was only a common peasant, a simple village craftsman; yet he was more regal than any king I have ever seen. And the child's mother – was she not queenly in her simple dignity? What, I asked myself, is the source of this inner nobility that can change peasants into royalty?"

King Balthasar walked to the entrance of his tent, looking up at the night sky crowded with stars. "I saw the  answer to my questions in the eyes of that infant. True nobility comes from an anointing of the heart, not of the head!" Quietly the king returned to his bed, and as he retired he thought to himself, "I am returning home by a different route and as a far different king. I rode to Bethlehem on my camel, high above the faceless sea of commoners, slaves and beggars, wondering about my kingship. I return home understanding that my camel drivers and every woman, man and child I saw along the way are royal persons deserving of my respect and honor. Indeed, that star was an omen of a new age. It has raised the curtain of history, not upon a revolution of slaves and servants overthrowing thrones; this is an evolution, as slaves and servants become equal to kings and queens!" As Balthasar blew out his oil lamp, he sighed, "Such an age is beyond imagination."

The three silk pavilions were raised and the camels bedded down as the noises of the caravan quieted on

the second night. Everyone had retired, and the last embers of the campfire glowed orange in the darkness. King Melchior stood outside his pavilion, holding an oblong ivory box encrusted with rare jewels. The three kings had ridden these past two days in silence, each one reflecting on the events in that little village of Bethlehem. What, indeed, had they seen in that poor, yet somehow sacred, stable?

LOOKING upward, King Melchior spoke, as if to the sky: "I followed one of your wondrous lights, hoping to find the answer to the most ancient of all riddles, the puzzle of life and death. My gift of myrrh was a sign of my inner quest. Myrrh is the ointment used for burial, and gifts tell a great deal about the giver. Ah yes, even kings die, no matter how great or powerful they are. Somewhere in this world, I thought, there must be a magic charm, a secret to escape death."

He opened the ivory box, removing a single yellow straw. "I was ashamed," he mused, "to tell the other two that I wanted to take a keepsake from that stable." For a long time he stood silent, looking at the straw he held. "I remember once reading a passage from one of their prophets of long ago; his name was Isaiah, as I recall. He promised a king to these people, and when he comes 'he will destroy death forever . . . and God will wipe away the tears from all faces . . . .' "

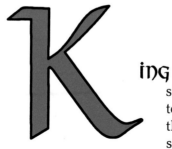**K**ing Melchior held the hollow straw up to his eye, pointing it toward the most brilliant star in the night sky. "Death, I now see, is like this straw — merely a passageway from one life to another. And we slip through as easily as my breath passes through this straw." Softly the wise man blew through his upraised straw.

At that moment King Caspar stepped out of the shadows, asking, "Melchior, old friend, what are you doing with that piece of straw? Are you practicing a new form of magic?"

"Oh, Caspar, what a start you gave me! This? It's a . . . that is, it's only a piece of . . . I took it from the stable back there in Bethlehem. I wanted something to remind me of what I saw there, the infant we came to adore. As I knelt before him, I saw something more than an infant with his two humble parents. I sensed an absence of fear in his mother and father, a sense of meaning in their simple lives. And in the child's eyes I saw the answer to a riddle that has given me no peace through all these many years."

Caspar chuckled. "Well, no fool like an old fool. Go to bed, friend, we have a hard ride ahead of us tomorrow." He laughed again gently. "A souvenir, you took a souvenir . . . ."

On the third night after the three silk pavilions had been erected and the camels fed and watered, the camp grew silent, as quiet as the vast sky above. King Caspar stood at the entrance of his tent watching the stars as they turned in their ancient orbits. "How strange," he

thought, "that we have ridden for three days without speaking to one another." He himself had said nothing more about his laughter the night before, nor had Melchior tried to explain why he had taken a souvenir from the stable.

Kin**g** Caspar took his leather saddlebag from inside his tent and opened a side pouch. He removed a silver flask inscribed with intricate hieroglyphics. Opening the flask and reverently placing it on the sand, he knelt before it. He made a profound bow and, after a few moments of silent adoration, he straightened but remained kneeling. Looking at the stars, he spoke: "I confess to you, I also took a souvenir from that stable. I came on this star-led adventure because I needed to find a God to believe in. My gift of incense, a traditional offering to the holy, was a telltale sign of my search for belief. Oh, I believed in some sort of impersonal divinity, but I could put no form or reason to it."

In the stillness, the silk cloth of the pavilion rustled softly. "I, the great Caspar," he spoke mockingly, "was the agnostic king. I came seeking a religious experience, some divine revelation. And my disappointment must have been the greatest as we entered that livestock stable. I was the last of the three to approach the infant to adore him. How un-godlike it was—the shabby stable, an infant lying in a bed of straw in a makeshift crib, his two peasant parents beside him. There were no heavenly lights, no divine thunder rumbled around us, no angelic music filled that stable. And my gift of incense in its golden chest seemed humorously out of place."

CASPAR removed a single yellow straw from the flask and bowed before it. "I am sorry I laughed at Melchior; I was laughing at myself, really, for I had also taken a souvenir from that place! I remember it as if it were this very night. How slowly I came forward to kneel before the infant! It seemed cruel to refuse to do so, an embarrassment to my two fellow kings, so I simply pretended adoration. Then that tiny baby looked at me. Everything and everyone there was suddenly bathed in light. There was a brilliance in those small eyes greater than the star we had followed. That stable had become more awesome than any great temple I had ever visited; everything, even the straw on the floor was aflame with glory. That's why I picked you up."

Leaving his tent, Caspar climbed to the top of a silent sand dune, and, looking up into the starry night, he raised his fragile straw to the heavens. "That child has come to end all religion and to make temples needless," he said. "Religion, by its name, is that which separates life from God. This child, I know, will someday bring together life and religion as one. Common and ordinary life will become sacred. There will be no need for temples." His arm swept outward to encompass the entire night sky. "This will be the Great Temple!"

Out of the shadows stepped Balthasar and Melchior, and the three stood without speaking, surrounded by the silence of the stars. Finally, King Balthasar said, "Each of us is going home a different way. We began our journey as men set apart by our regal birth, by our priestly knowledge, different from the common people we encountered. Noble companions, we have ridden three

days now from Bethlehem. Did we find what we came seeking? If so, how has our view of life changed?" For a long time the three kings stood silent. Then they began to speak, each in turn.

"I, Balthasar, have seen the beginning of a new age, the end of a time when only a select few are given reverence, treated as gods come to earth. I have seen the end to kings and queens as the anointed ones, for now every person will be seen as royal, unique and possessed of great dignity."

"I, Melchior, have seen the death of death. Now I see only life in countless forms of transformation."

"And I, Caspar, what have I seen? I have seen God, and now I see God everywhere!"

THE FIFTH YARN

CHRIS CARPENTER

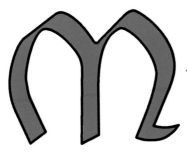

MANY YEARS AGO in the small town of Bethlehem, deep in the hill country of the Missouri Ozarks, there lived a truly talented furniture maker named Chris Carpenter. He was known throughout the area for his beautiful oak furniture. Examples of his artistic work could be found in the homes of the simple as well as the rich and influential.

The local banker had commissioned Chris to make him a large oak desk for his office in the Bethlehem bank. More than large, it was massive and made of *solid* oak. When Chris delivered the desk, he knocked 30% off the agreed-upon price. "A professional discount," the furniture maker said. The banker, always happy to make money, smiled and was grateful. 30% *is* 30%, even if in his heart, the banker didn't consider the town's cabinetmaker and carpenter to be a professional in the same league with himself.

The county judge had Chris make him a large floor-to-ceiling bookcase for his law office. The judge was well-known in the county for his vast library of philosophical books. He was, as the town folks said, "A liberal thinker." The judge didn't attend church, except for funerals or weddings, since he considered religion necessary only for the poor and uneducated. As with the banker, Chris extended a 30% discount to the judge as a professional courtesy.

The local parish church also had an example of the carpenter's artistic work. The parish priest had commissioned Chris to build a large wooden pulpit, designed by the pastor himself. The beautifully carved oak pulpit was an impressive artistic addition to the small parish church. It rose above the congregation like the conning tower of a giant submarine cutting through a sea of nodding heads. When the priest preached, he looked like a U-boat captain shouting orders and firing theological torpedoes at various social Good Ship Lollipops.

When Chris delivered the pulpit to the church, the priest talked on and on about how this new pulpit would give glory and praise to God. He must have mentioned "God" at least twenty times as he praised the carpenter for his work. Chris got the hint and cut 50% off the bill "as a donation, Father, to the Church." The big discount made the priest twice as pleased with the new pulpit.

These are but three examples of Chris's artistry and generosity; there are many more. The poor folks also had their samples of his work in their homes: a cradle, a porch swing or a fine oak hat tree for the hallway. For the poor farmers Chris did his work in exchange for a ham or some flour – or sometimes for no more than the cost of the wood.

One warm day near the end of September, as the oak trees of the Ozarks were turning color, Chris dropped by the town's tavern. He mentioned to some friends there that this Christmas he was inviting all of his friends and customers to see his work – and a few to a special "Christmas House." A woman at the bar named Rhonda asked, "Is that where you display things you make so people can purchased them as gifts for Christmas?" Chris only smiled and replied, "Just come and see."

Over the rest of autumn, Chris wasn't seen much in town. The gossip around the town square was that he was busy making things for his Christmas House. The cabinetmaker lived on a farm several miles outside of Bethlehem, and even when friends stopped by to visit, the gate was closed. On the gate was a sign that read, "Come back again. Sorry, I'm busy."

ℕOW, in the middle of December, the banker, the judge and the parish priest received a special party invitation. Also invited was Rhonda, the barmaid at the town's tavern. Rhonda had dyed red hair and had been married four times, legally. Three of her friends, known locally as "the cowboys," also got invitations to Chris's Christmas House. The three men really weren't cowboys, since there were no cattle ranches around Bethlehem, Missouri. They were simple, unmarried farm hands who dressed in western clothing and cowboy boots. They were, however, as loud, rough and dirty as cowboys who had just come off a trail drive.

The invitation that the seven received read as follows:

**You are kindly invited to attend
the Grand Opening
of the Bethlehem Christmas House
at my farm on Millwood Road
on December 24, at 10:00 p.m.**

R.S.V.P. (only if you're not coming)

Chris Carpenter

Neither the banker, the judge nor the parish priest had any desire to attend the carpenter's Christmas House — whatever that was. When they heard that Rhonda and the cowboys also had been invited, their desire to attend shrank to zero. Now, the banker, judge and parish priest would have sent their regrets, except that each was indebted to the furniture maker for his generosity to them. Christmas Eve or not, they felt obligated to go out to his farm and see whatever this Christmas House was.

As for Rhonda and the cowboys, lacking families to be with on Christmas Eve, they were delighted to be invited to Chris's farm. Unlike the other three, Rhonda and the cowboys were really curious about what their friend had been doing for the past two months.

On Christmas Eve the ground was covered by a light snow, and the night sky was crowded with bright stars. The banker, judge and parish priest arrived first and parked in the barnyard. Each of them arrived in their own cars. Rhonda and the cowboys arrived last and came roaring into the barnyard in a broken down pickup truck, the four of them squeezed into the front seat. The farmhouse and barn were dark, except for a large electric star on top of the barn. A lone yellow glowing oil lantern hung over the barn door. From inside came the sound of Christmas carols.

Finally, Chris opened the barn door. "Welcome, friends. Thank you for coming. I've been looking forward to tonight for weeks. I want to share with you my secret discovery for how to make Christmas truly Christmas. Please, each of you come into my magical, merry Christmas House."

**S**lowly the seven guests entered the mystery-shrouded barn. They stood in total darkness waiting as the music of *O, Come, All Ye Faithful* filled the air already rich with the smell of hay and horses. Suddenly, the barn was illuminated by giant spider-like webs made up of a maze of crossing strands of colored Christmas tree lights. The seven stood silent and open-mouthed at what they saw.

In the center of the barn was a large oak table and eight oak chairs. The seven guests were welded to the floor in amazement as they gazed at the table and chairs. What held them all in tongue-tied disbelief wasn't simply the workmanship of the furniture—even though it was magnificent—it was the *size* of the table and chairs. They were gigantic!

The table must have stood at least eighteen feet high! It would have taken three men standing on each other's shoulders to reach the top of the table. It must have been a good sixty feet in length, extending all the way back into the shadowy area in the darkened part of the barn. The eight beautifully carved oak chairs measured at least thirteen feet just to the seats. From the ground it appeared that there were plates, knives and forks on the table, and the guests could smell roast beef on platters that were not visible from floor level.

The cabinetmaker broke the spell. "Come, friends, join me for a Christmas Eve supper." Reaching up, Chris grabbed the lower rung on one of the eight chairs and swung himself up to reach the next rung. He proceeded to climb up to the seat of the chair by using the rungs on the side of the chair like a ladder. Once there, he called for the others to follow.

Dumbfounded and bewildered, the other guests looked at one another. Then, breaking out into snickers, and obviously having fun, the three cowboys boosted Rhonda up to reach the first rung of her chair and scrambled up the sides of theirs. The banker, judge and priest, not without some difficulty, made their way up to the seats of their chairs.

As they took their places at the great table, they found that they could hardly see over the top of the table. In front of them were giant wooden plates, with huge knives and forks to match. In the center of the table were heaps of rich food: roast beef, potatoes, gravy and other delights that gave off wonderful aromas. With disbelief, the guests examined their wooden plates, which must have been two feet in diameter. The giant wooden spoons were so large that it was difficult to imagine how one could get any food into one's mouth with them.

Chris bowed his head, saying, "Let us pray...." He pronounced the blessing prayer with words about peace on earth and joy to all. As he prayed, the banker shot an angry glance at the judge, and together they stared at the priest. The look that the three exchanged said, "This is madness! How do we get out of here?"

Meanwhile the other four, with bowed heads and folded hands, were lost in the beauty of Chris's meal blessing. When the prayer ended, Rhonda and the three cowboys picked up their forks and began waving them with glee. Indeed, the four of them had imbibed a bit of Christmas Cheer in the pickup as they drove out to the farm – Jack Daniel's Black Label – but it was more than that. This was fun! Whatever was in the air, it was wonderful. The night, however, was far from wonderful for the priest, banker and judge. They felt stupid and ridiculous to be perched like midgets on highchairs in this madman's Yuletide fun house.

"Mr. Carpenter!" shouted the banker, struggling to look powerful and important as he peered over the top of his plate, "I...we, my two friends and I, don't find your little joke to be funny. We're all busy men. We have obligations. Father, here, has important matters to attend to on this Christmas Eve."

"Yes," spoke up the priest, grateful to the banker for providing him with an excuse to leave. "There will be last-minute confessions to be heard – and Midnight Mass preparations. Oh, yes, I'm far too busy to stay...."

"I too have other obligations," snapped the judge as he and the other two began to climb down from their chairs on their way out the door. "Good night to all of you."

Chris looked down the long Christmas table and said to Rhonda and the three cowboys, "And you, friends, would you also like to leave?"

"Hell, *no!*" sang out Rhonda, her red dyed hair sparkling in the light of the towering candles on the table. "This is wild, man! Right, guys? No, we're staying – that is, if you'll have us."

Chris smiled a grin as big as his wooden plate, and Rhonda continued, "It's crazy. I mean these big chairs and this tall table, even the spoons: all this stuff is so big! It makes you feel like you're a kid again at your folks's table. You feel so small and yet...ah...taken care of, if you know what I mean."

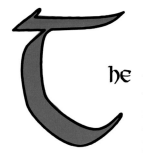he three cowboys, having taken off their cowboy hats, were nodding in agreement as Rhonda continued, "All this makes you feel like somewhere . . . ," as she spoke she leaned her head way back and gazed up into the darkened high rafters of the barn, ". . . somewhere, someone is taking care of you. You know, someone real big, big enough to have made this table and chairs."

"Yeah," said one of the cowboys, "Rhonda's right. We're so small next to this big furniture, and yet it isn't bad. It's kind'a fun."

"Right," added Rhonda, "and I don't know about you guys, but I got this feeling that if I ate at a table like this, no matter what my problems were, somehow they would be taken care of. Know what I mean? Like any moment, your dad or mom is gonna' lean over you and cut your meat into little pieces so you can chew it."

"Come on, follow me," said Chris as he climbed up on top of the giant oak table. The other four followed as he began walking down the long table toward the far end which was lost in the darkness. When they reached the end of the table, the cabinet maker pulled on a rope. Slowly, the large hayloft door at the peak of the barn swung upward, revealing an awesome sight. Before them was framed the crystal clear winter night sky filled with stars!

Rhonda and the cowboys stood with arms around one another, looking out at the Christmas Eve night sky. From where they stood in the open hayloft doorway, the earth below wasn't visible. All they could see was the star-clustered universe which was stunning, more spectacular than a Midnight Mass in any great cathedral. The stars suspended in stillness were more powerful than Handel's *Messiah* sung by a choir of thousands. Their experience just heightened what they had felt when they were seated at Chris's Christmas table, a sense of being so small, yet neither alone nor vulnerable in their smallness.

The four silently looked out at the star-filled heavens as if they were astronauts standing together at the open bay door of a space station orbiting earth. Rhonda put what they were all thinking into words.

"Chris, you may be crazy, but one thing's for sure. Regardless of what the banker or the priest said . . . ." Her voice trailed off as she turned around and realized that she and the cowboys were alone. Chris Carpenter was nowhere to be seen. Rhonda turned again to face the crisp night sky and took a deep breath. With her arms around the three cowboys, she said with a cute nod of her head, "You know what, guys? It's just like they say, 'Christmas is only for kids.' "

the sixth yarn

SANTA'S GIFT

'Τ WAS TWO WEEKS BEFORE Christmas and the North Pole home of Santa Claus was full of activity. Great white clouds of steam rose from the tall smokestacks of the toy factory into the snow-filled air. Inside, elves worked night and day to complete the toys that Santa would soon give to the children of the world.

A knock came at the kitchen door of Santa's home. When Mrs. Claus opened the door, she found a delegation of elves standing in the yellow light that flooded out from the open door. "Hello," said Mrs. Claus. "What can I do for you?"

"Hello, Mrs. Claus," said an elf named Gransen.

Knowing that Gransen was the foreman at the toy factory, Mrs. Claus's heart skipped a beat. For a split second she thought to herself, "Oh no, not a breakdown at this time of year. It's only two weeks till Christmas!"

But she was soon relieved, for he continued, "We've come to ask your help. We would like to give Santa Claus a gift this year, but we don't know what to give him. He seems to have everything.

"He's always so jolly when he comes to visit the

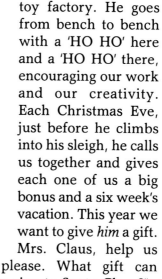

toy factory. He goes from bench to bench with a 'HO HO' here and a 'HO HO' there, encouraging our work and our creativity. Each Christmas Eve, just before he climbs into his sleigh, he calls us together and gives each one of us a big bonus and a six week's vacation. This year we want to give *him* a gift. Mrs. Claus, help us please. What gift can we give to Santa Claus?"

"Right now I can't think of a thing," said Mrs. Claus. "You will have to let me think about your request. That's my problem too—not only every Christmas but on his birthday as well. He doesn't want any new clothing. You know, he's worn that same red suit every day for hundreds of years now! He's a simple man with simple needs. I don't know what you can give him. But let me think about it." So the elves returned to the toy factory and Mrs. Claus to preparing dinner.

That evening after their dinner, as Santa was studying a collection of huge maps of the world, Mrs. Claus said, "Santa, you must find that midnight ride difficult. You're not as young as you used to be. As the population of the world grows, you have to keep adding new addresses to your list. And there are new streets to find and all those new homes to visit. You must be tired at just the thought of that long trip."

"Yes, dear," sighed Santa. "It isn't easy."

"What if this year," said Mrs. Claus, "as a gift from all of us here at the North Pole, maybe the elves and I could take your place and give the gifts to the children?"

"**A**bsolutely impossible," said Santa. "We must not forget tradition, dear. The children don't expect to see Mrs. Claus coming down the chimney! And think of all the disappointment if a team of little elves were to take my place. The children do love them, but on Christmas Eve they want Santa Claus to visit them. No, no, no, thank you for the thought, dear, but the children want to see *me*. It's my vocation, and, difficult or not, I must carry out the Christmas tradition."

The next morning Mrs. Claus visited the toy factory and told the elves what Santa had said about her only idea. The elves all shook their heads sadly. But Gransen said, "Perhaps we need to give him a magical gift."

"A magical gift for Santa?" asked Mrs. Claus. "What do

you mean?"

"Let us think about it," the elves said. They waved good-bye as they returned to their work benches, talking amongst themselves.

Two weeks later, after dark on Christmas Eve, Santa's great sleigh was parked in front of the house with the reindeer all harnessed. The tiny silver bells on the harnesses jingled in the crisp night air as all the elves from the North Pole Toy Factory arrived at Santa's home.

The elves knocked, and Santa called out, "HO HO, come in." As they opened the door, they saw him standing by the fire filling his great bag with toys and gifts.

"Merry Christmas, my friends! Well, I'm all ready to go. HO HO HO! Look out there at the falling snow. It's going to be a great night for the trip. HO HO HO!"

The crowd of elves only smiled and nodded. Then Gransen stepped forward and said, "Santa Claus, we have a gift for you."

"HO HO HO, for *me*? You have a gift for Santa Claus? HO HO HO . . . ." And Santa roared with laughter. But inside, Santa was a bit frightened, for he didn't know what that meant. "Little friends," he said, "I *give* gifts — that's who I *am*. I don't *receive* gifts! Besides, I don't *need* anything."

Gransen just smiled and winked. As he did, the elves pulled a toy sled into Santa's house on which sat a

beautifully wrapped present! The elves all applauded loudly and cried out for Santa to open his Christmas present.

Now, Santa didn't know what to do. For all these hundreds of years, if you can believe it, he had never unwrapped a gift! Santa only *gave* gifts, so he was quite embarrassed and awkward as he began to unwrap his first Christmas gift.

With the elves crowded around him, Santa untied the ribbon, tore off the wrapping and opened the box. When he looked inside, his face became full of puzzlement, for the box was completely empty! "HO, ho, ho . . ." Santa's jolly laughter melted away like snow on a hot kitchen stove. "I don't understand," said Santa. "There's nothing in here!"

"Because we love you, Santa," said Gransen, "we've given you the one gift you truly need – nothing! It's a magical gift. Your gift box is full of the precious gift of emptiness."

Santa Claus looked at his gift of emptiness, and fear howled like a timber wolf in his heart. For Santa, to be empty was to be needy. Ever since he was a child, Santa had feared being needy, for who loves a needy person? People seem to love only those who are full of talents and can do many things!

Santa looked again at his gift of emptiness and shook

his great white head in confusion. Gransen said, "The gift of emptiness is to be needy in a way that isn't bad, Santa. Emptiness is an enchanted, hollow space that we all need in our hearts. Even you, Santa, the world's most generous giver of gifts, need to have an enchanted place in your heart that only another or others can fill." As he finished speaking, all the elves nodded in silent agreement. Mrs. Claus wiped a single tear from her eye with a corner of her apron.

There was a long silence in which Santa slowly began to understand his Christmas gift. How can anyone, even Santa Claus, celebrate Christmas unless there is in his or her heart an emptiness, a hollow place that needs filling? Then he understood: to be empty isn't a fault that one tries to hide for fear of looking weak. In his emptiness Santa felt the joy and eagerness of anticipation. Emptiness, he thought, is the one condition that is absolutely necessary to truly taste the feast of Christmas!

 **S** Mrs. Claus embraced him and the elves jumped up and down, shouting with joy, tears flowed down Santa's face, for his heart was as full to bursting as his great toy bag. "Come on," cried Santa, wiping the tears from his cheeks with a sweep of his sleeve. "Hurry, dear, get your fur coat. And all of you, my good little friends, you too! Let's all ride together in the sleigh tonight. This Christmas Eve let's all deliver the gifts and share our joy on this most holy and magical of nights!"

the
seventh yarn

the
heart house

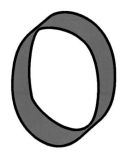**NCE UPON A TIME** there was a house shaped exactly like a human heart. It was two stories high and had a brick chimney. The Heart House also had a large front door, but the door had no knob on the outside and could only be opened from the inside. The Heart House only opened its door on certain rare occasions to let someone in. This fact shouldn't be too surprising, however, since it was an ordinary Heart House and didn't have a lot of room inside.

Birthdays and anniversaries were special days during the year when the Heart House opened its front door, but they were nothing at all compared to what happened on December 25! With a cheery "Merry Christmas," the door would swing wide open and out would come a shower of beautifully wrapped gifts. The flood of gifts would delight the friends of the Heart House and cause it to hop up and down with pride and joy.

Yet each time that its door would suddenly open for gifts to pour out, the Heart House always closed it again quickly. This was a good habit it had learned as a child from its parents. "Don't leave your front door open, dear," they had warned frequently, "who knows what kind of person or thing might wander in?"

Although it was located on a nice street in a lovely part of town, the Heart House wasn't happy. It did enjoy wrapping presents and giving gifts, but the joy didn't last. Longing for fulfillment, the Heart House had attended all kinds of workshops and seminars on happiness. It had even taken a three-week course called "The Open

Door Movement." While it had learned a lot of techniques on how to open one's door more often, how to have a pleasant threshold, the Heart House found that childhood patterns are difficult to break.

As a result, except for the gift-giving times, the Heart House kept its front door securely closed. This house rule was especially true in the case of visitors who appeared uncouth, who looked like they might track in mud on the rugs or swing from the drapes. The most impolite were guests who rearranged furniture without even asking permission. The Heart House loved a well-ordered, neat, clean house with everything in its proper place.

When it heard someone knocking at its door, the Heart would peek out the single small upstairs window to see who was down below. If the visitor had muddy feet or appeared to be the type that liked to rearrange furniture, the Heart pretended not to be at home.

he weeks just before Christmas were especially busy for the Heart House. Christmas gift catalogs had to be read and visits made to shops and stores. The Heart House found it great fun to shop for gifts and to wrap them in colorful paper.

Now, one night, less than a week before Christmas, as the snow lay deep on the earth and the full moon ice-skated on the top of snowdrifts, a knock came at the front door of the Heart House. "Go away," said the Heart House, "I'm busy wrapping Christmas gifts."

Again, there was a knock, this time louder than before. "Who's there?" asked the Heart House. No reply came, only a much larger knock. So the Heart looked out the small upstairs window to see who was at its front door. Wonder of wonders, it was a little elf! From the Heart's point of view, however, it was a very large elf, much too large to let inside. "What do you want?" asked the Heart House from the small upstairs window.

"I'm with the Santa Claus group, but I got separated from the others at the last rest stop. When I came out of the restroom, the sleigh, reindeer, elf helpers, Santa — the whole show — had left without me. I realize that I'm not one of the important elves. I guess they just didn't miss me. I've been walking for miles, and it's so cold out here. I saw the smoke rising from your chimney, and it looked warm inside. Could I come in and warm myself by your fire?"

"You're too big for my little Heart House! Besides, you look like the type who likes to rearrange furniture."

"Oh, no, never," replied the elf, "I'm not that kind of person, and I don't have muddy feet either. I know that you're not a large Heart House and that there's not room for all of me inside, but couldn't I at least put my feet inside to get my toes warm?"

long pause followed this request as the Heart was in inner turmoil over whether to let someone potentially dangerous inside. Finally, opening its front door, it said, "Well, all right, you can put your feet inside, but I don't have time to visit. I'm far too busy wrapping gifts for Christmas."

"I only want to warm my toes," said the elf, sliding his long legs inside the house until his toes were up against the old wood-burning stove. "Ah, that feels wonderful!"

The Heart House made no reply but only hummed a Christmas song as it prepared for its big give-away on December 25.

"Beautiful gifts," said the elf, "look expensive."

"Yes, they are beautiful and some are expensive. I like to give the biggest and best gifts I can," replied the Heart House.

"Would you like to give the best gift in all the world, the most adventuresome and exciting of all gifts?" asked the elf with a big grin.

"I've been to every shopping mall in town, to every

gift shop and department store, but I've never seen a gift that sounds that special. Tell me, what is it?"

"Give away your *front door*!"

"What? Are you crazy? My front door?"

"Yes, tear it off its hinges. Not only is it the best gift in the world, it's the secret of Christmas. Gift-giving implies being willing to receive as well as give. Gifts change people, but most folks don't like to be changed by others. It feels good to see others influenced by your gifts, but most people don't like to be changed themselves!

"Your front door swings outward in giving, but you prevent gifts from coming to you by closing your door right after you've given your gifts. Christmas is a risky time if you're open to receiving gifts as much as giving them!"

"But if I no longer have a front door, then . . . . "

 **es,** I realize there's a danger. People can come in and rearrange your furniture, make your life different and even more difficult. If you can take the risk, however, then you will never become an old house. By staying open to being changed, you will be gifted with countless new ideas and untold possibilities."

The elf turned his head slightly and listened, "Hear what I hear?"

he Heart House listened too. On the crisp night air, far-off in the distance, he could hear the jingling of sleigh bells. They grew louder until suddenly there was a pawing of hooves and sleigh runners screeching to a stop on the roof of the Heart House.

"Ah, looks like I've been missed," said the elf with a laugh. "Merry Christmas, and thanks for letting me warm my toes while Santa and the gang returned to find me."

Three days later on Christmas, the Heart House rang out a loud "Merry Christmas." Then, with great apprehension, it tore off its front door and gave it away! It was the best gift it had ever given and one that certainly changed its life. From that Christmas day on, the Heart House grew larger and larger until it became the biggest and happiest Heart House in all the land.

he old white-bearded Christmas Eve Storyteller leaned back in his chair and closed his eyes. As I looked around the room, I noticed that my sister's eyes were also closed. She had a smile on her face, as if images from the tales were still dancing in her head. My two little brothers were both sound asleep, one in each of my parents' laps. Halfway through the long evening, they had climbed up there to nest.

The Storyteller's hands lay folded on his lap, resting after an evening of spinning yarns. He had woven together a colorful tapestry which, many years later, I realized contained the many and beautiful themes of Christmas.

That Christmas tapestry of tales, woven long ago, has hung on the wall of my heart since I was a child. Each Christmas Eve I again sit before it and reverently finger its colorful yarns. In the process, as if by magic, the yarns speak, and I hear again the waltz-like voice of the Storyteller. And, as on that Christmas Eve night long ago, I can hear again the crackle of the fire as it once again sings, "Child, fear not the storm outside! You are safe in this warm circle of love."

the end